Jumbled

Written by Jasmine Richards

Illustrated by Zavian Archibald

Collins

Chapter 1

Omari wasn't in a rush to get to school. He normally loved school. He loved maths. He loved art. He even loved rainy playtimes. But he didn't love the idea of doing a presentation to his class today.

"Why are you walking so slowly?" Omari's mum asked him. "It's almost like you're moving backwards. You'll need back-to-front shoes like a douen!"

"A douen?" Omari repeated. "What's that?"

"Haven't you read about them yet in your great-granny's journal?" Mum asked. "A douen is a type of jumbie – you remember, it's that creature from Caribbean folk tales that likes to play pranks and raid gardens," Mum smiled. "It's in the journal. You did remember to pack it?"

Omari patted the school bag hanging off his shoulder. "I've got Great-Granny's journal. My presentation about folk tales would be even worse without it," he sighed.

Mum lifted his chin. "Don't be nervous, you'll do brilliantly. Your great-granny spent a long time writing down these folk stories. She didn't want us to ever forget that jumbies exist. Or what tricks they can play."

"You don't actually believe in jumbies, do you, Mum?" Omari asked.

Mum looked embarrassed. "Of course not, but stories of jumbies are told across the whole of the Caribbean." She shrugged. "People swear that they've seen the massacooramaan, the river jumbie who capsizes boats, and the lagahoo, who can shapeshift into different animals, tiny or huge. Then there's the very naughty baccoo, who loves bananas. You wouldn't want to spot him on a walk."

Omari wrinkled his nose. He thought the stories were a bit silly. Jumbies didn't exist.

"Promise me that you'll be careful with the journal?" Mum asked Omari as they arrived at the school gates. "We don't own many things that belonged to your great-granny."

"I promise," Omari said. "I've even put my banana in the front bit of my bag away from it. No squashed snacks today."

He waved goodbye to his mum.

Omari trudged into school. His friend Will was waiting for him.

"Hurry up!" Will said. Omari could tell Will was excited about giving his presentation.

Omari couldn't understand it. "Won't you get nervous when you get up in front of the class and start talking?" he asked.

"Who says I'm talking!?"
Will replied. "I'll be *singing* my
presentation on goblins."

Omari raised an eyebrow.
He was pretty sure their teacher,
Mr Dawkins, wasn't going to be
impressed by a song about goblins.
Everyone knew that Will wanted
to be a singer when he grew up.
He always found a way to turn his
homework into a performance.

"Because you're my best
friend, I won't make you wait,"
Will said. "I'll sing the song to you
right now!"

*"Goblin, goblin, I can see
Hiding low or by a tree.
Friend or foe, it's not always clear,
Humans, listen, don't go near."*

Will then started to dance like
a goblin. Which meant swinging
his arms. A lot.

Chapter 2

The bell rang for the start of school.

Omari was relieved. He had a feeling that Will's
goblin song had another verse. He and Will raced into
their classroom. Mr Dawkins was sitting in the corner.
His looked like he was staring into space, but he was
also snoring.

Strange, Omari thought.

Standing at the front of the class was a different teacher that Omari had never seen before. He was rather small and had long arms, sharp teeth and very large eyes.

He pointed a long finger at Omari and Will. "You're late," he said.

Omari tried to apologise but the teacher shook his head. "I was just stating facts. I don't actually care. I'm Mr Boya. I'm looking after the class today."

Mr Boya perched on the desk. He picked up
a nearby orange and took a bite. It wasn't peeled.
The teacher spat out a pip and then started eating
an apple. Even the core and the stem!

"Are you hungry, sir?" Will asked, as he and Omari
sat at their table.

"Extremely," replied Mr Boya. "But this fruit
is disgusting. I'd much prefer a banana. And milk.
Where's the milk?"

The class looked at each other.

"Um, we don't have any milk," Will said.

"What?" boomed Mr Boya. "I came here for milk!
I thought schools loved giving that stuff out?"

Omari shook his head. He looked at Will. What was
going on with this new teacher – and what was wrong
with Mr Dawkins? He glanced over, but their usual
teacher was still snoring.

"Now I'm very unhappy," Mr Boya said. "Someone cheer me up!"

"I can tell you a joke," Josie said, and jumped to her feet. She almost knocked over the shallow box on her desk, which held a miniature sand pyramid and sphinx.

It must be for Josie's presentation, thought Omari.

Mr Boya picked an apple seed from between his very sharp-looking teeth. "I'm listening," he said.

Josie grinned. Omari knew she loved telling jokes, but she never normally got to in class.

"Why did the chicken cross the road?" Josie asked.

Mr Boya shrugged. "Because it was being chased by a ravenous creature who never feels full?"

Josie gulped. "Um, no, it was trying to get to the other side." She frowned. "It's a pretty basic joke, but I've got better ones."

Mr Boya sniffed. "Tell me another animal joke. I'm a great fan of animals. All animals. Especially if I can eat them with hot pepper sauce."

Josie frowned but went on. "OK … why did the duck cross the road?" She didn't wait for a reply. "Because it thought it was a chicken."

Mr Boya didn't smile.

"OK," Josie said. "Why did the dinosaur cross the road? Because the chicken wasn't around yet!"

Mr Boya groaned loudly. "Next!"

Chapter 3

The teacher pointed at Omari. "How about you? Entertain me."

Omari stood up. Why did Mr Boya have to choose him? "Erm, I'm not great with stuff like this … but my friend Will has got a brilliant song about goblins."

"Goblins are the worst," Mr Boya sneered. "So chatty and friendly. I don't want to hear about them. I want to hear from you."

"OK." Omari took Great-Granny's notebook out of his bag. "I can tell you about jumbies – "

Mr Boya gasped and sat up a bit straighter.
He looked worried.

That's strange, Omari thought.

"My great-granny was from the Caribbean,"
Omari explained to his class. "She liked telling stories,
just like her mother did – my great-great-granny.
The stories were often about jumbies. There are lots
of islands in the Caribbean, and most islands have
a version of a jumbie. You need to be very careful
around these creatures."

Omari turned a page. "One kind of jumbie is the lagahoo. He's a shapeshifter. The lagahoo might sometimes choose to help you and other times not. It kind of depends."

Mr Boya snorted. "That one just helps himself to your dinner. Trust me." Mr Boya slapped a hand over his mouth as if he shouldn't have said that.

"In Guyana, you have something called a baccoo," Omari went on. "It has very big eyes and very long arms."

"A bit like you, Mr Boya!" Josie joked.

"Don't be ridiculous!" Mr Boya said, crossing his dangly arms in a huff.

"A baccoo likes throwing stones at houses,"
Omari went on. "It also loves moving things about
and making you think you've lost things."

"This baccoo guy sounds like fun, if you ask me,"
Mr Boya said. "What's wrong with a few games?
Everyone loves games."

Mr Dawkins suddenly gave a loud snort, and the class turned to look at him.

Their teacher was still snoring even though his eyes were open. Now he was dribbling a bit too.

Omari went back to the journal. "A baccoo's favourite food – " he started to say. His hands trembled as he read the rest of the words. "Its favourite food is – "

"Milk and bananas."

The whole class gasped. Will nudged Omari.

"Mr Boya is a baccoo," he hissed.

"I know!" Omari whispered back.

Omari looked down at the journal once more.
What were they going to do? Maybe his great-granny's
stories could help them?

"Sometimes a baccoo can even grant wishes,"
Omari read, "but only if it's happy with you."

Chapter 4

He looked up. The baccoo didn't look happy enough to grant wishes. Then Omari remembered he had a banana in the front of his bag! He took it out and gave it a good sniff so the baccoo would see it. "Yum," Omari said.

The creature's eyes went wide. "That looks rather delicious," he said.

"Does it?" said Omari. "I wish I could give it to you, but I'm going to need something in return."

"What?" asked the baccoo, licking his lips.

"We're going to need our teacher back," Omari said.

The baccoo frowned. "I like being your teacher. Even if you don't have milk!" He shook his head. "I'm not waking Mr Sleepyhead up. Not even for a banana." The baccoo laughed. "There's nothing you can do about it. I can't be defeated."

Omari looked down at
the journal again. There was something
scribbled in tiny letters at the bottom of
the page, so small that, at first, he thought
it was just a mistake. It read: "baccoos
really don't like sand."

He turned around to Josie, whose
pyramid was still sitting in front of her.
She had sand!

"Can I borrow your
presentation, Josie?" Omari whispered.

Josie shrugged. "Sure."

Omari picked it up carefully and
walked towards the baccoo. "Have you
seen Josie's project, Mr Boya?
Isn't it cool? Look at all the tiny grains
of sand!" He thrust the box out in front
of him.

The baccoo leapt off the table and
edged towards the door. "Get that sand
away from me!"

"Only if you wake up Mr Dawkins
and leave us alone!" said Omari.

"Fine," the baccoo growled. He threw an orange at Mr Dawkins and the teacher started blinking in his chair.

"Was I sleeping?" their teacher asked.

Omari tossed the banana to the baccoo as he ran from the classroom. "Have a snack for the way home."

The door slammed behind him, and the class cheered.

"Why are you cheering?" Mr Dawkins asked. "What did I miss?"

"Omari did a great presentation," Josie said. "Now we know how to defeat a baccoo!"

Omari grinned. "All thanks to my great-granny!"

"Very good," said Mr Dawkins. "Who'd like to go next?"

Will stood up. "Who wants to hear my song? It's about goblins."

Omari groaned, but he got ready to listen. Anything was better than being taught by a jumbie!

Writing to Great-Granny

Great-Granny,
I know you're not with us anymore to see it, but I thought I'd better add to your journal. Who knows? Maybe my great-grandchildren will read it one day.

Actually, great-grandchildren, if you're reading this: jumbies EXIST! They really do. I thought it was all made up, but I was wrong. Really wrong. A jumbie came to my class today. It was a baccoo and he called himself Mr Boya.

Baccoos are really sneaky and like playing tricks on people. They love milk and bananas and hate sand.

I've been doing a bit more research and, apparently, lots of jumbies hate sand because they can't help but count every grain. It's a jumbie thing. Strange, huh?

No wonder the jumbie in my class ran off when I brought over that pyramid. Imagine how boring it would be to count all that sand!

Until next time,
Omari

 Ideas for reading

Written by Gill Matthews
Primary Literacy Consultant

Reading objectives:
- ask questions to improve their understanding of a text
- draw inferences such as inferring characters' feelings, thoughts and motives from their actions, and justify inferences with evidence
- predict what might happen from details stated and implied

Spoken language objectives:
- articulate and justify answers, arguments and opinions
- give well-structured descriptions, explanations and narratives for different purposes, including for expressing feelings
- participate in discussions, presentations, performances, role play, improvisations and debates

Curriculum links: Geography – Locational knowledge

Interest words: trembled, gasped, hissed

Resources: IT, atlas

Build a context for reading
- Ask children to look at the front cover and to read the title. Ask what they think "jumbled" means and what they think is happening in the illustration.
- Read the back-cover blurb. Discuss what this tells the children about the front cover and what they think might happen in the story.
- Point out that this is a fantasy story. Explore children's experience of fantasy stories and establish some of the typical features of the genre.

Understand and apply reading strategies
- Read pp2–9 aloud, using appropriate expression. Ask the children how they think Omari is feeling. Ask whether they think Mum does believe in jumbies. Encourage them to support their responses with reasons and evidence from the text.
- Ask children to read pp10–19. Discuss the new teacher. Who, or what, do the children think he is? What do they think is going to happen next?